THE
DARK LADY

JANICE GREENE

SADDLEBACK
EDUCATIONAL PUBLISHING

▊QUICKREADS

SERIES 1

Black Widow Beauty
Danger on Ice
Empty Eyes
The Experiment
The Kula'i Street Knights
The Mystery Quilt
No Way to Run
The Ritual
The 75-Cent Son
The Very Bad Dream

SERIES 2

The Accuser
Ben Cody's Treasure
Blackout
The Eye of the Hurricane
The House on the Hill
Look to the Light
Ring of Fear
The Tiger Lily Code
Tug-of-War
The White Room

SERIES 3

The Bad Luck Play
Breaking Point
Death Grip
Fat Boy
No Exit
No Place Like Home
The Plot
Something Dreadful Down Below
Sounds of Terror
The Woman Who Loved a Ghost

SERIES 4

The Barge Ghost
Beasts
Blood and Basketball
Bus 99
The Dark Lady
Dimes to Dollars
Read My Lips
Ruby's Terrible Secret
Student Bodies
Tough Girl

SADDLEBACK
EDUCATIONAL PUBLISHING
www.sdlback.com

ISBN-13: 978-1-61651-215-6
ISBN-10: 1-61651-215-6
eBook: 978-1-60291-937-2

Printed in Guangzhou, China
0311/03-150-11

15 14 13 12 11   2 3 4 5 6

■ ■ ■

Andrew hurried down the narrow aisle of the crowded plane. "How are we doing, Jenny?"

His pretty assistant bent over her clipboard. "All the musicians are on board," she reported.

"Even the viola players?" Andrew interrupted her nervously.

"Yes, even the viola players," she assured him. "They caught that last taxi, remember?"

"And the crew?" Andrew went on.

Jenny nodded. "The crew's on board. All the husbands and wives and kids are here. The whole symphony orchestra's here—all 152 of us! So sit down and relax."

Andrew sank back in his seat and snapped on his seatbelt. "This tour's a disaster already," he muttered.

"This tour is *not* a disaster," Jenny said consolingly.

"We barely made it out of San Francisco on time," he groaned. "We have to be in Jerusalem in just 20 hours. I have no idea how we're going to manage nine cities."

"Don't be such a worrywart. You've got me, remember?" Jenny chirped.

Andrew managed a little smile. "I know. But for some reason I just have a bad feeling about this tour."

"You *always* have bad feelings," Jenny reminded him. "And right now you're wound up tighter than a yo-yo. Want a neck rub?"

"Please," Andrew sighed. He leaned forward and moaned as he felt Jenny's small, strong fingers on his neck.

Then his cell phone rang.

"*Arrrgh!*" he cried out as he pulled the phone from his pocket.

"Andrew? It's Ken," a voice said.

It was Andrew's roommate.

"Hey, someone left a weird phone message for you," Ken went on.

"What? What did the message say?" Andrew asked.

"The guy said that The Dark Lady belongs to him," Ken said.

"You're kidding!" Andrew wailed.

Just then a small, plump man clutching a violin case appeared in front of Andrew. Next to him stood an exasperated flight attendant.

Andrew looked up and gritted his teeth. "Phillip," he said. "I'm on the phone. Jenny can help you."

"I don't want your *assistant*. I want you," Phillip insisted.

"Can't it wait?" Andrew asked.

"No, it cannot," Phillip snapped.

"Ken," Andrew said into the phone, "I'll call you back in five minutes." Then he turned to Phillip.

"This *woman*," Phillip sputtered, "says I can't hold my violin in my lap." He glared at the flight attendant.

"If he won't use the overhead bin," she explained, "he can just slip it under the seat in front of him."

"Listen to her!" Phillip hissed. "She wants me to put my violin on the *floor*. She obviously doesn't know that this violin is The Dark Lady."

The flight attendant looked blank.

Phillip shook his head in disgust. "It's only one of the most famous violins in the world!" He glowered at the attendant until she shrugged and walked away.

"Can you *believe* this?" Phillip cried.

"Phillip, it's for your own safety," Andrew said. "If the plane crashed, it could fly out of your hands."

"Nonsense," Phillip said. "I'd *never* let go of The Dark Lady."

"Then put your coat over your lap and hide it," Andrew whispered.

"That awful woman's going to be very suspicious," Phillip whined.

"No. That woman is *tired* of you, Phillip. She'll leave you alone—trust me," Andrew said as Phillip huffed off.

Andrew punched in Ken's number. "Can you remember *exactly* what the message was?" he asked.

Ken paused a moment. "He said, 'The Dark Lady is mine.' That's it. Then he hung up," he said. "You're taking The Dark Lady on the tour, right?"

"Unfortunately, yes," Andrew said. "Phillip insisted."

"You better keep an eye on it," Ken suggested before he hung up.

Jenny was curious. "What was that all about?" she asked.

Andrew glanced around the crowded airplane. "I don't want to talk here," he whispered.

Suddenly two slim fingers tapped Andrew on the shoulder. He looked up impatiently, but smiled when he saw Nineve, Phillip's wife.

Andrew took her hand. "You look wonderful, as always," he said, admiring her elegant dress.

"Thank you, dear," Nineve said. "I hope Phillip wasn't too difficult. He gets so anxious, you know."

"No problem," Andrew shrugged.

Nineve shook her head, smiling. "He won't set that violin down for an instant," she said. "If he gets up for anything, *I* have to hold it. Traveling with a baby would be easier."

"I could hold it," Andrew offered.

Nineve smiled warmly. "Thank you, dear. Isaac volunteered, too. But for some reason it has to be me."

All passengers must take their seats as we prepare for takeoff, a voice announced over the P.A. system .

Nineve waved a graceful goodbye. "I'd better go," she said.

Jenny looked at Andrew. "You have a crush on her, don't you?"

Andrew smiled. "We're all in love with Nineve—every guy in the whole symphony. How on earth does Phillip deserve her?"

"No justice?" Jenny suggested.

Andrew nodded. "If there was any justice,

Isaac would be the star, and Phillip would be number two."

"In your dreams," Jenny laughed. "Dealing with Phillip is half your job. Want a pillow? You should sleep. In a few hours we arrive in Jerusalem."

"I *am* wiped out," Andrew admitted as he took a pillow from Jenny.

Andrew was just drifting off when he remembered the e-mail he had downloaded just before getting on the plane. He got out his laptop and found a few messages from friends, and a lot of spam. Then he noticed one subject line: *Dark Lady*. The sender was *SmarterThanU*. He opened the message and read:

```
Before you leave Jerusalem,
The Dark Lady will be mine.
```

■ ■ ■

Andrew was anxious to talk to Jenny, but she was sleeping. More than an assistant, she was a friend. And he needed a friend right now. He didn't really trust anyone but Jenny.

For the next several hours, Andrew stared into space. *Who had sent him the message? What in the world was he going to do about it?*

His mind went around in circles. Finally, his eyelids drooped, and he sank into the pillow. Then he heard the announcement: the airplane would be landing in 15 minutes.

"Wake up, Jenny. We're in Paris," Andrew said.

"How long before we catch the next plane?" she yawned. "I want to hear about that phone call."

"We'll have an hour there," he said. "Let's take a walk in the airport and I'll tell you about it."

But just as the plane landed, a worried-looking trombone player hurried over. He'd left some music at home. Could he have the fax number of the hotel, so his daughter could fax him the music? Then Phillip and Nineve appeared. Phillip couldn't bear airplane food. Could Andrew help them find something decent to eat in the airport? His talk with

Jenny would have to wait.

They looked at seven restaurants. Phillip rejected every one. Finally, Jenny grumbled, "We better find our gate or we'll miss our connection."

To get to their gate, they had to pass through security once more. There they joined a long, slow-moving line of people waiting to be checked.

"All this security is *insane!*" Phillip complained angrily.

People in uniform were now checking purses and jackets and bags. "Open, please," a man said, pointing to Phillip's violin case.

Keeping the case very close to him, Phillip slowly opened it.

People around him went silent as they saw the violin. Its finish was unusual—a brown so dark that it was nearly black. It reminded Andrew of a deep pool, so deep it went on forever.

"*Tres belle*," murmured the man in uniform. *Very beautiful.*

Phillip snapped the case shut and

immediately hugged it to his chest.

As they boarded their flight, Jenny urged Andrew to get some sleep. "We'll be very busy when we land."

Jenny dozed off almost immediately. Andrew closed his eyes and worried about herding 152 people to the hotel. Then he worried about the second plane. Its cargo included 36 trunks of clothes and 72 trunks of instruments. These, too, had to get to the hotel. Andrew stayed awake and fretted.

When they landed in Jerusalem, Andrew couldn't stop yawning. He was hoping to share a taxi with Jenny. But Phillip insisted that he ride to the hotel with him and Nineve.

Nineve looked around. "Where's your sweetheart, Andrew?" she asked, as they stepped outside.

Andrew blushed. "Jenny? We're just friends," he said.

"I think you could be more than just friends," Nineve said with a smile.

"Oh, I don't know," he said. "She's probably got a boyfriend back in San Francisco."

"Well, don't you sell yourself short!" Nineve exclaimed. "You're a great guy, and any girl would be lucky to have you in her life."

Hmmm, I wonder if she's right? Andrew thought to himself. Then he said aloud, "So, Nineve, do you think—"

Then, impatient at being ignored, Phillip interrupted him. "Just how secure is this hotel, Andrew?" he fussed. "I'm concerned about the safety of my violin."

Andrew sighed. "I'm told it's very safe," he assured Phillip. "The Israelis are famous for their security, you know."

But Andrew felt a knot of worry in his stomach. The threatening words of the e-mail came back to him:

```
Before you leave Jerusalem,
The Dark Lady will be mine.
```

■ ■ ■

By the time they checked into the hotel, Andrew was so tired his hand shook as he signed his name.

There was no time for him to rest. A viola player had brought his wife and two sons. But the hotel had given him a room with a single bed. A trombone was delivered to a percussionist's room. And Phillip wouldn't leave him alone. "My room isn't next to yours!" he whined. "I want you close by in case I need you."

You want me close by so you can drive me crazy, Andrew thought. "I'll take care of it as soon as I can," he said. He tried to speak pleasantly, but he could hear the sharpness in his voice. Andrew was relieved when Nineve took Phillip's arm. "Let's just give Andrew a little peace now, dear," she murmured.

Finally, he was alone in his room.

Andrew flopped down on the bed and closed his eyes. He had to get some rest before tomorrow's rehearsal.

Hearing a knock on the door, he flew upright. If it was Phillip, he was ready to punch him. It was Isaac.

Isaac was young, blond, and movie-star handsome. He smiled apologetically. "Sorry

14

to bother you, Andrew. I just wanted you to know I've switched rooms with Phillip. So he's next to you now."

"Thanks, Isaac," Andrew said. "That will sure be a big help."

Isaac smiled sympathetically, "Well," he said, "when Phillip's happy, we're all happy, right?"

"Right," Andrew agreed.

Just then, Jenny appeared in the doorway. "Hey, guys," she said.

"Hey, cutie," Isaac said. He put an arm around Jenny's shoulders and kissed the top of her head.

Andrew felt a twinge of jealousy, which surprised him. "Jenny and I have to go out now," he said to Isaac. "See you in the morning, okay?"

■ ■ ■

Andrew and Jenny stopped at a falafel stand down the street from the hotel. Andrew had always enjoyed the fried balls of garbanzo beans wrapped in pita bread.

But falafel in Jerusalem was something else! The stand had more than a dozen items one could put in a falafel—cabbage, all kinds of peppers, fried eggplant, radish, spicy pickles, and so on.

"Fantastic!" Andrew said happily.

"I love this hot sauce," Jenny said, wiping away a few tears. "Now, tell me what's going on."

He did, ending with, "I can't believe any member of the symphony would have sent those messages."

"I don't understand why someone would steal The Dark Lady," Jenny mused. "It couldn't be played in public. It's too famous."

"Right," Andrew said. "The thieves would have to sell it."

Jenny nodded. "I agree that no one in the symphony would steal The Dark Lady. That violin is too special to all of us. But if it's not one of the musicians, who could it be?"

Andrew had no answer.

They walked back to the hotel and said

goodnight. Andrew tumbled into bed and fell asleep in seconds.

■ ■ ■

When he heard a loud crash, Andrew wondered if he'd been dreaming. But then he heard a heavy thud from the room next door—Phillip and Nineve's room.

He jumped up and ran out to the hallway, and fumbled at the door. *"Phillip!"* he called out.

"Help me!" Phillip moaned.

The door was unlocked. The room was dark when Andrew stepped inside. Suddenly, someone lunged forward and wrapped gloved fingers around his neck. He struggled, gasping.

"Turn on the light! Where's the light?" Nineve called out.

"Police! *Police!*" Phillip shrieked.

Finally, Andrew was able to grab his assailant's wrist and hold on. A gloved fist struck his face again and again. But he didn't let go—until a bright light exploded in his head, and then everything went dark.

When he opened his eyes again, Andrew was lying on a bed. He felt a throbbing pain in his head.

Clare, the symphony doctor, smiled down at him. "Poor Andrew! You're going to look pretty beat up for the next few days," she said.

"I *feel* beat up," Andrew groaned.

Phillip was sitting on a couch, The Dark Lady held against his chest. Nineve was beside him, looking tense. A policeman stood nearby.

"This is Officer Kalman. He wants to talk to you," the doctor said.

Officer Kalman was tan and fit-looking in a crisp uniform. He looked at Andrew with a touch of pity. "Can we speak in private?" he asked.

Andrew nodded. The two men slowly walked back to his room and sat down.

"Please tell me everything that happened to you," Officer Kalman said. His pen was poised over a small notepad.

Andrew told the story quickly. There wasn't that much to tell.

At one point, the police officer interrupted. "You say you had to pull the assailant's fingers away from your throat? Wasn't that a terribly difficult thing to do?"

Andrew thought about it. "Not that hard, I guess," he said.

"Are you a strong person? Do you lift weights?" Officer Kalman asked.

"No," Andrew said. "So maybe the fellow wasn't all that strong himself."

Officer Kalman raised an eyebrow. "Maybe it was someone who didn't want to strain his fingers," he said. "Perhaps one of the musicians in your symphony. By the way—how much is the violin worth?" he asked.

Andrew tried to shrug, but a stab of pain stopped him. "Who knows? Millions. I'd say at least six million dollars."

"Just one more thing, sir. How long has this famous violin belonged to Phillip?" Officer Kalman asked.

"He's had it about a year and a half,"

Andrew estimated. "Actually, the violin *doesn't* belong to Phillip. It's really owned by the symphony."

Again, Officer Kalman's eyebrow went up. "Is that so? And who would play this violin if something happened to Phillip?"

Andrew gasped. "Are you saying someone tried to *murder* Phillip?" he cried. "That's hard to believe!"

"I'm just looking at all possible motives," Officer Kalman said quickly. "Theft is surely a possibility. But murder is a possibility also. So can you tell me who—?"

"It would be Isaac," Andrew said.

"I will interview him also," Officer Kalman said, springing easily to his feet. "Obviously, you need some rest now, sir. Good night."

You mean good morning, Andrew answered silently. The clock said 4:14. He had to be up in three hours. He lay back on the bed, groaning.

■ ■ ■

When someone pounded on the door before 7:00, Andrew got up. His mind was still foggy from painkillers.

It was Phillip, his pudgy face pink. "We must come up with a plan of action," he said. "We can't have any more of these—uh, incidents."

Andrew grunted in reply.

Nineve peeked around Phillip. "You must feel awful, Andrew," she said. "I'm so sorry." She gave his hand a gentle squeeze. "Come to our room and have some toast and coffee with us."

She led Andrew into the room. He couldn't help noticing the large bouquet of roses on an end table.

"Isaac sent them," Nineve said. "To cheer us up. Aren't they lovely?"

Andrew felt a twinge of jealousy. He knew that he was good with people. But Isaac had *class*. Then they heard a knock on the door.

"Hi, it's me," Jenny said. Her face went

white when she saw Andrew. "What did Clare say? Are you going to be all right?"

"It's not serious," Andrew said.

Phillip was annoyed. "Excuse me, Jenny," he said. "Nineve and I have some important things to discuss with Andrew just now."

"*Phillip* . . .!" Jenny objected.

"It's okay, Phillip," Andrew said. "I'll come up with a plan."

"Oh, look at the time!" Nineve said. "We should leave for the concert hall in twenty minutes."

Someone else knocked on the door as Andrew was hungrily wolfing down a piece of toast.

"Andrew! I've been looking for you." It was Michael, one of the violinists. His son had broken a tooth and needed to see a dentist right away.

Sarah, one of the bass players, was with him. She couldn't find the stool she sat on when she played.

Andrew grabbed a second piece of toast. He and Jenny headed out the door. "Thanks for breakfast," he said to Nineve. "See you at rehearsal."

Before leaving, Andrew checked his cell phone. Oh, no! There was a text message from *SmarterThanU*:

> I'm everywhere. But you'll never see me.

■ ■ ■

By the time Andrew and Jenny arrived at the concert hall, rehearsal had already started. So had a fight.

"I do *not* play duets!" Phillip yelled. Under the stage spotlight, his plump face looked pink and shiny.

Eric, the orchestra conductor, was exasperated. "I'm sure you and Isaac will sound wonderful together. Please try it—*just once*—and see for yourself!"

"I do *not* play with second-rate violinists!" Phillip fumed.

Eric's voice was acid. "Isaac could join a number of other symphonies and be a *star*, Phillip," he snarled. "Why he remains with us is a mystery—and a blessing." With that, he tipped an imaginary hat to Isaac.

Isaac smiled modestly. "Oh, let him play it as a solo," he said. "It really does sound better that way."

Eric wasn't convinced. "Well, if you really think so," he finally agreed.

Phillip threw up his hands. "*Of course* it sounds better," he crowed.

Andrew turned to Jenny. "How can he be so agreeable?" he said. "If I were Isaac, I'd have punched Phillip a long time ago."

"Me, too," Jenny said with a laugh. "Isaac is really amazing, isn't he!"

Andrew stole a glance at Jenny. Seeing the glow on her face as she looked at Isaac, he'd felt a twinge of jealousy. "Yeah, just amazing," he replied sarcastically.

Jenny studied Andrew's face, surprised at his tone. She started to say something, but then Phillip stepped to the front of the stage. All eyes turned to him when he lifted his bow to the violin.

Phillip began to play. At first the music

seemed light and carefree. It reminded Andrew of a spring night. Then it sounded like mighty winds blowing black clouds around. As always, Andrew was swept away by the power of Phillip's artistry. Or was it the power of The Dark Lady? He never knew for sure.

In the violin section, Michael was trying to control a cough.

Phillip stopped playing. "Stop it! That coughing is driving me insane."

"Sorry," Michael said. "Anybody have some cough drops?"

"I do," Isaac said. "In my jacket."

Andrew got up to get them. He trotted backstage and quickly found Isaac's jacket. It was a new one—very expensive-looking. Part of being classy, Andrew sighed. In one pocket was a hotel key. In the other, Andrew found cough drops—and a silver earring shaped like a rose.

Jenny— Andrew thought. He was sure it belonged to her. He felt a flush of unreasonable anger. It wasn't that he was in love with her. But why did she have to fall for *Isaac*?

Andrew sat down just as Phillip began to play once more. In spite of the cough drop, Michael went on coughing.

Phillip stopped playing. "This is absolutely *intolerable!*" he shrieked.

"Everyone—except Phillip—take a ten-minute break," Eric said.

The players got up and headed out into the warm sunshine.

As they left the building, Andrew asked if Jenny was missing an earring. His voice sounded snide and bitter.

Jenny stared at him, taken aback by his tone. "No," she said. "Why?"

"There's a silver earring in Isaac's pocket. It's shaped like a rose," Andrew said accusingly.

They stared at each other. "I think it's Nineve's," Jenny said quietly.

Eric tapped the music stand with his baton. "All right, Phillip. Here's your chance. Now you can play for ten minutes in absolute peace."

As Phillip lifted his bow, Andrew saw a small cloud of dust drift down on the little violinist.

Andrew got up and walked toward the stage. He looked up at the rows of lights hanging from the ceiling. Someone was moving on the catwalk between the lights!

"GET BACK!" he yelled to Phillip.

Startled, Phillip stepped back.

Like a falling tree, a heavy row of lights came crashing to the stage! A cloud of gray dust rose from the floor. Andrew was relieved to see that Phillip was unhurt.

He glanced at Jenny. "You take the right," he said as he headed left.

Backstage, Andrew opened the door to a dressing room. Immediately, he sensed movement behind him! He started to turn when a strong arm gripped his neck and the sharp blade of a knife touched his cheek!

"Sorry, Andrew," Isaac muttered.

Along with a jolt of fear, Andrew felt a

27

tearing regret that he'd never see Jenny again.

Then Eric and Jenny rushed into the room. "*No!*" Jenny cried out.

Isaac froze. Then, suddenly, a dozen or more people were in the room, too—horn players, bass players, and violinists. They all stared, wide-eyed, at Andrew and Isaac.

"Let us in!" Phillip's voice piped up as he and Nineve tried to push their way through the crowd.

Isaac was trembling. The knife clattered to the floor. "It was Nineve," he blurted out. "She planned it all."

Nineve's face went white.

"We'll check your laptop, Nineve," Jenny said. "And your jewelry—for a missing earring."

"It was all her idea. She's guilty, believe me!" Isaac cried out.

"*I* believe you," Phillip said sadly. The light was gone from his eyes as he looked at his wife. "You were never mine," he added mournfully.

"*Never!*" Nineve hissed. "Of course Isaac wanted the violin and the fame. But mostly, he wanted *me*, Phillip. So I played him—just as expertly as you played The Dark Lady."

Then Nineve sneered at all of them. Andrew was shocked to see such an ugly look on a face he had thought to be so beautiful.

■ ■ ■

Even hours later, everything that had happened seemed unreal to Andrew. Everything except Jenny.

Now he put his hand on her cheek.

She smiled and leaned forward slowly, expectantly. They kissed.

Andrew took her in his arms.

"I didn't know you cared," Jenny said, half-laughing.

"*I'm* the one who didn't know anything," Andrew whispered.

"We need to make up for lost time," Jenny said, and they kissed again.

■ ■ ■

The concert hall was crowded and humming with voices.

Then the house lights dimmed and the red velvet curtain rose gracefully upward. The symphony members were all seated and ready. Michael was in Isaac's place.

Phillip came forward for his solo. His puffy eyes made him look older. For once, Andrew felt a stab of sympathy for the fussy little man. He reached for Jenny's hand.

Phillip began to play. The sound was deep, rich, and almost unbearably sad. A woman in the front row dabbed at her eyes with a tissue.

Then the full symphony joined in. Andrew yawned. Jenny squeezed his hand and smiled. At last he knew that they'd make it through the rest of the tour—somehow. He closed his eyes and slept like a child.

After-Reading Wrap-Up

1. At the beginning of the story, why did Jenny call Andrew a "worrywart"? What were some of his concerns?

2. Phillip had a lot of trouble getting along with people. Name two characters he clashed with, and describe his problem with each of them.

3. For most of the story, Isaac appeared to be a handsome, gracious fellow. What later events in the story revealed a very different side of his personality?

4. Andrew envied Isaac for having "class." What did Andrew observe to come to this conclusion?

5. What did Andrew think when he found the earring in the pocket of Isaac's jacket? What did her find out later about the earring?

6. By the end of the story, Andrew's opinion of Nineve had radically changed. What did he originally think of her? What did her think later on?